U0063762

新雅兒童英文圖解字典
片語動詞

Elaine Tin　著

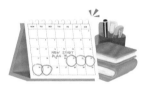

carry out
執行

hand in
提交

新雅文化事業有限公司
www.sunya.com.hk

如何使用新雅點讀筆閱讀本書？

新雅·點讀樂園 升級功能

讓孩子學習更輕鬆愉快！

本系列屬「新雅點讀樂園」產品之一，若配備新雅點讀筆，孩子可以點讀書中的字詞和相關例句的內容，聆聽英語和粵語，或是英語和普通話的發音。

想了解更多「新雅點讀樂園」產品，請瀏覽新雅網頁（www.sunya.com.hk）或掃描右邊的QR code進入 新雅·點讀樂園 。

Sun
太陽

1. 下載本書的點讀筆檔案

1 瀏覽新雅網頁(www.sunya.com.hk) 或掃描右邊的 QR code 進入 新雅•點讀樂園 。

2 點選 下載點讀筆檔案 ▶ 。

3 依照下載區的步驟說明，點選及下載《新雅兒童英文圖解字典》的點讀筆檔案至電腦，並複製至新雅點讀筆的「BOOKS」資料夾內。

2. 啟動點讀功能

開啟點讀筆後，請點選封面右上角的 新雅•點讀樂園 圖示，然後便可翻開書本，點選書本上字詞、圖畫或句子，點讀筆便會播放相應的內容。

3. 選擇語言

如想切換播放語言，請點選內頁右上角的圖示，當再次點選內頁時，點讀筆便會使用所選的語言播放點選的內容。

如何使用本字典?

　　《新雅兒童英文圖解字典:片語動詞》適合幼稚園至初小學生,收錄超過360個片語動詞。每個詞目均附中文釋義、漢語拼音、雙語例句,並配以精美插圖,內容清楚,一目了然。

全書把片語動詞按英文字母順序排列,方便學童查閱,節省時間。

中文釋義上方提供漢語拼音,幫助孩子學習中文字詞的漢語發音。

利用新雅點讀筆點選圖示,可切換播放語言。

B

ENG × 粵語　ENG × 普通話

bring back
dài huí lái
帶回來

43

例句

We brought back many strawberries that we had picked on the farm.
我們帶了很多在農場摘的士多啤梨回來。

strawberry的普通話是「草莓」。

英文例句示範詞目的正確用法,中文翻譯方便讀者掌握意思。

鑑於粵普用字略有不同,為便利孩子學習,本書會按需提供粵普詞彙對照。

本書為入門級的片語動詞字典，旨在幫助學童掌握詞目的基本釋義，並建立其英文詞彙量。在內容編排上，本書精選幼稚園至初小程度必學及常用的片語動詞，一個單頁呈現一個詞目，幫助孩子輕鬆學習，逐步擴闊詞彙量。

有些片語動詞一詞多義，用法甚廣。本書作為初階字典，按讀者程度精選和收錄相關釋義，並以上標數字區分詞條。另鼓勵讀者參考例句，配合語境，理解各詞目的語義和實際用法。

由於部分片語動詞需符合特定情境才可使用，故此本字典會按需提供文字說明。此字框另會收載額外語文知識，以便學童全面掌握片語動詞的應用。

目錄

C

✦ R

✦ S

abide by

zūn shǒu
遵守

 例句

All library users must abide by the library rules.

所有圖書館使用者必須遵守圖書館規則。

act as

dān rèn
擔任

例句 ----------------------------

My dad acts as our coach when I play football with my friends.

我和朋友踢足球時，爸爸擔任我們的教練。

act out

xíng wéi shī dàng

行為失當

例句

Billy always acts out when he is unhappy.

比利不高興時，就會做出搗蛋調皮的行為。

add up to

zǒng gòng shì
總共是

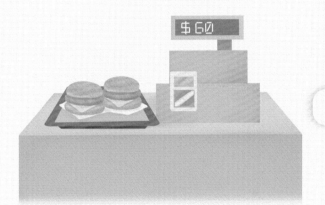

19

 例句 --------------------------

Two hamburgers add up to sixty dollars.

兩個漢堡包合共六十元。

agree with

<ruby>適<rt>shì</rt></ruby><ruby>合<rt>hé</rt></ruby>

20

 例句 -

It seems the new job agrees with you.
You look a lot happier now.

新工作似乎很適合你，你看起來愉快多了。

aim at

zhǐ zài

旨在

例句 -

The game aims at developing children's spelling skills.

這個遊戲旨在培養小朋友的拼字技巧。

allow for

gù jí

顧及

 例句 -----------------------------

We should buy smaller chairs to allow for the height of the children.

我們應該顧及孩子的身高，購買小一點的椅子。

answer back

dǐng zuǐ
頂嘴

 例句 -

Mrs Chan felt angry that her son was answering her back.

兒子在頂嘴，令陳太太感到很生氣。

answer for

fù zé
負責

 例句 -

The moving company has to answer for the damage to the furniture.

搬運公司要為家具損壞負責。

A

ask after

wèn hòu
問候

How are your parents?

 例句 ----------------------------

I ran into our old neighbour Mr Chan yesterday. He asked after my parents.

昨天我碰到舊鄰居陳先生，他向我的父母問好。

ask for

<ruby>要<rt>yāo</rt></ruby><ruby>求<rt>qiú</rt></ruby>

例句

The guest is asking for an extra blanket.
住客要求額外一張毛毯。

back away

hòu tuì
後退

 例句 ------------------------------

The man saw a ferocious dog and backed away.

男士看見一隻兇猛的狗,嚇得向後退。

back down

rèn cuò
認錯

28

 例句 -

He backed down and apologised for his rude behaviour.

他為自己無禮的行為認錯和道歉。

back out

shí yán

食言

 例句 -

He said he would ride the roller coaster with me but he backed out at the last minute.

他說他會和我坐過山車，但是他在最後一刻食言了。

back up

bèi fèn

備份

例句

The technician backs up the files to the hard disk every day.

技術員每天都把檔案備份到硬碟上。

be carried away

xīng fèn wàng xíng

興奮忘形

 例句 --------------------------------

We were carried away when playing in the inflatable castle.

我們在充氣城堡玩得樂極忘形。

bear with

nài xīn děng dài
耐心等待

例句

Please bear with me while I get you the menu.

請耐心等待，我給你去拿菜單。

believe in

xìn fèng

信奉

 例句 ----------------------------

He believes in ghosts and he has to sleep with the lights on.

他相信有鬼,睡覺時要亮着燈。

belong to

shǔ yú
屬於

 例句 -

This pencil case belongs to Sammy.

這個筆盒屬於森美。

blow away

lìng rén jīng xǐ
令人驚喜

35

 例句 --------------------------------

His magic tricks blew the children away.
他的魔術表演令孩子們很驚喜。

blow out

<ruby>吹<rt>chuī</rt></ruby><ruby>滅<rt>miè</rt></ruby>

36

 例句 -------------------------------

She blew out all the candles in one breath.

她一口氣吹滅了所有蠟燭。

blow up¹

chōng qì
充氣

例句 -

Dad is blowing up the basketball with a pump.

爸爸正在用氣泵為籃球充氣。

blow up²

jí dù fèn nù
極度憤怒

38

 例句

The coach blew up at Terry because he was late for two hours.

教練對泰利大發雷霆，因為他遲到了兩個小時。

break down

gù   zhàng
故障

 例句 -

The vacuum cleaner has broken down.
We need to sweep the floor with the
broom.

吸塵機壞了，我們要用掃帚來掃地。

break into

chuǎng jìn

闖進

40

 例句

Two masked men broke into a big house to steal valuables.

兩名蒙面男子闖進一所大屋，盜竊貴重物品。

break up

fēn shǒu
分手

 例句 ------------------------------

Jimmy is so sad because his girlfriend has just broken up with him.

占美很傷心，因為女朋友剛剛和他分手。

bring along

xié dài
攜帶

 例句 -----------------------

The little girl brings along her favourite doll wherever she goes.

無論到哪裏去，小女孩都會帶着她最喜愛的洋娃娃。

bring back

dài huí lái

帶回來

例句 -

We brought back many strawberries that we had picked on the farm.

我們帶了很多在農場摘的士多啤梨回來。

strawberry的普通話是「草莓」。

bring out

tū xiǎn
突顯

44

 例句

The red lanterns at the door bring out the festive cheer.

門口的紅色燈籠突顯了節日的喜慶氣氛。

bring together

lìng rén tuán jié
令人團結

 例句 --------------------------

The orienteering has brought the boys together.

野外定向令這羣男孩團結起來。

bring up¹

yǎng yù
養育

 例句 -

You have to be very patient to bring up children.

養育孩子需要很有耐性。

bring up²

tí chū huà tí
提出（話題）

47

例句 --------------------------------

During the meeting, the manager brought up the issue of energy saving.

在會議上，經理提出節約能源的議題。

buckle up

kòu shàng　　ān quán dài
扣上（安全帶）

48

  例句 ------------------------------

Dad helps me buckle up the seat belt.

爸爸幫我扣上安全帶。

burn down

shāo huǐ
燒毀

例句

The factory was burned down in an accident.

工廠在一場意外中被燒毀。

burn out

pí láo guò dù
疲勞過度

50

 例句 -

After working day and night, he finally burned himself out.

他日以繼夜地工作，最終累垮了自己。

burn up

fā gāo shāo
發高燒

例句

The baby is burning up. His parents are worried about him badly.

嬰兒發高燒，他的父母很擔心他。

burst out
<ruby>突<rt>tū</rt></ruby> <ruby>然<rt>rán</rt></ruby> <ruby>大<rt>dà</rt></ruby> <ruby>喊<rt>hǎn</rt></ruby>
突然大喊

Watch out!

52

 例句

"Watch out!" dad burst out when he saw a bike coming.

爸爸看到單車騎過來時，大喊：「小心！」

bike的普通話是「自行車」。

call back

huí bō diàn huà
回撥電話

 例句 --------------------------

I am busy right now. Let me call you back later.

我正在忙着，稍後回撥電話給你吧。

call off

qǔ xiāo
取消

 例句 ----------------------------

We have to call off the outing to the park because of the bad weather.

由於天氣惡劣，我們只好取消到公園郊遊。

call on

hào zhào

號召

例句 -

The teacher called on the students to arrange the chairs.

老師號召學生把椅子排列好。

calm down

<ruby>冷<rt>lěng</rt> 靜<rt>jìng</rt></ruby>

 例句

She is calming herself down by taking a deep breath.

她深呼吸一下，讓自己冷靜下來。

care for

xǐ huan
喜歡

例句 --------------------------

No, thanks. I do not really care for chocolate.

不用了，謝謝。我不太喜歡巧克力。

carry on

jì xù

繼續

 例句 --------------------------

He got up from the fall and carried on running.

他跌倒後站起來，繼續向前跑。

carry out

zhí xíng

執行

 例句 -

From today on, I will carry out this new study plan.

由今天開始，我會執行這個新的學習計劃。

catch on

biàn de liú xíng
變得流行

60

例句 --------------------------

Nutritious smoothies have caught on with people who want to lose weight.

營養豐富的奶昔很受減重人士歡迎。

cater for

yíng hé
迎合

VEGETARIAN MENU

 例句 -

This restaurant provides a separate menu to cater for vegetarians.

這間餐廳另設菜單，以迎合素食者。

change over

gēng huàn
更換

例句

We have changed over from a mechanical lock to an electronic lock.

我們把機械鎖更換成電子鎖。

check in

bàn lǐ rù zhù shǒu xù
辦理入住手續

 例句

check in 的相反詞是 check out，
指「辦理退房手續」。

The doorman showed us where to check in.

酒店門衞告訴我們在哪裏辦理入住手續。

ENG × 粵語

ENG × 普通話

check off

dǎ gōu
打勾

 例句 - - - - - -

check off 多用於核對事項，表示正確或已處理。

Mum is checking off the items which she has already put in the trolley.

媽媽正在核對已放進手推車的物品，在清單上打勾。

check up on

<ruby>檢<rt>jiǎn</rt></ruby><ruby>視<rt>shì</rt></ruby>

檢視

 例句 ----------------------------

The doctor comes to the ward regularly to check up on his patients.

醫生定時來到病房，檢視病人的情況。

cheer up

gāo xìng qǐ lái
高興起來

 例句 -

The teacher is cheering the new kid up with a hand puppet.

老師用手偶讓這位新來的孩子高興起來。

66

chip in

còu qián

湊錢

 例句

The sisters chipped in to buy a doll house.

姊妹湊錢購買一座娃娃屋。

clean up

qīng jié
清潔

 例句

The kids cleaned themselves up after playing in the sandpit.

孩子們在沙池玩耍後，把自己清潔乾淨。

clean up after

wéi bié rén qīng lǐ
為別人清理

 例句 ----------------------------

Dog owners should always clean up after their dogs.

每當狗隻便溺後，狗主都應該為牠們清理排泄物。

clear up[1]

qīng lǐ
清理

 例句 - - - -

clear up 多指清理地方或物品。

The students are clearing up the tables.

學生正在清理桌子。

clear up²

tiān qì zhuǎn qíng
天氣轉晴

 例句 ----------------------------

Let's play football if the weather clears up.

如果天氣轉晴，我們去踢足球吧。

close down

<ruby>倒<rt>dǎo</rt></ruby> <ruby>閉<rt>bì</rt></ruby>

倒閉

 例句 ----------------------------

Too bad! My favourite toy store has closed down.

真可惜！我最喜愛的玩具店倒閉了。

come across

ǒu rán fā xiàn
偶然發現

 例句 -

I came across a dog which was on a leash. It might be a missing dog.

我碰見了一隻繫上狗帶的狗，牠可能走失了。

come away

_{diào xià}
掉下

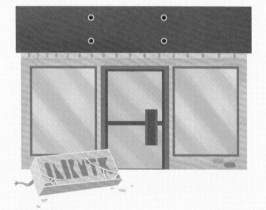

74

例句 --------------------------------

The signboard came away from the wall.

招牌從牆上掉下來了。

come back

huí lái
回來

 例句 -

Uncle Sam came back from Australia to visit us.

森叔叔從澳洲回來探望我們。

C

come before

yōu xiān yú
優先於

例句

Safety comes before everything. Always wear a helmet.

安全至上。請務必佩戴頭盔。

come between

pò huài guān xì
破壞關係

例句

Although we both want to win, we never let the competition come between us.

雖然我們都想勝出,但是我們不會讓比賽破壞彼此的關係。

come forward

zhàn chū lái
站出來

78

例句

come forward 多用於
主動提供協助或資訊。

Mr Wong came forward and told the police who the pickpocket was.

黃先生挺身而出，告訴警察誰是小偷。

come from

_{lái} _{zì}
來自

 例句

Yoko is our new classmate who comes from Japan.

洋子是來自日本的新同學。

come in

jìn lái
進來

 例句 -

Come in, please.

請進來。

come over

sì hū shì
似乎是

例句 --------------------------------

Although he is a superstar, he comes over very friendly.

雖然他是超級巨星，但是他似乎為人很友善。

come up with

xiǎng chū

想出

例句 ----------------------------

He came up with a good idea to display his guitars.

他想出了一個好方法來陳列結他。

consist of

zǔ chéng
組成

 例句

Our band consists of a vocalist, a guitarist and a keyboard player.

我們的樂隊由一個主唱、一個結他手和一個琴鍵手組成。

ENG × 粵語

ENG × 普通話

cool off

liáng kuai xià lái
涼快下來

84

 例句 ------------------------------

Take a mini fan with you so that you can cool yourself off anytime.

帶上迷你電風扇吧，這樣你就可以隨時涼快下來。

count down

<ruby>倒<rt>dào</rt></ruby><ruby>數<rt>shǔ</rt></ruby>

倒數

85

She is counting down to her birthday.

她正在倒數自己的生日。

count in

bāo kuò   mǒu rén
包括（某人）

 例句 -

Are you going to play Chinese chequers? Count me in!

你們要玩跳棋嗎？算上我吧！

count on

<ruby>指<rt>zhǐ</rt></ruby> <ruby>望<rt>wàng</rt></ruby>

指望

 例句 --------------------------------

He is the best player on our team. We count on him to win the game.

他是我們球隊中的最佳球員。我們指望他
為球隊取勝。

count out

bù bāo kuò mǒu rén
不包括（某人）

 例句 ------------------------------

I do not swim. Please count me out.

我不懂得游泳，請不要算上我。

ENG × 粵語

ENG × 普通話

cover up

yǐn mán
隱瞞

例句

He failed the test and tried to cover it up.

他測驗不及格，嘗試隱瞞起來。

crack down

yán lì dǎ jī
嚴厲打擊

90

例句 -

The police are cracking down on jaywalking.

警方正在嚴厲打擊亂過馬路。

cross out

huà xiàn shān chú
畫線刪除

 例句 ----------------------------

Please cross out the inapplicable options.

請畫線刪除不適用的選項。

cry out

dà jiào

大叫

 例句

My little sister cried out in fear when she saw a mouse.

妹妹看見老鼠時，嚇得大叫起來。

cuddle up

yī wēi
依偎

 例句 -

My mum and I are cuddling up and reading the book together.

媽媽和我正在依偎在一起看書。

cut back

jiǎn shǎo
減少

 例句

You should cut back on the amount you spend on clothes.

你應該減少花費金錢在服裝上。

cut in

chā zuǐ
插嘴

例句

"Let's take a photo!" Hannah cut in while we were talking.

我們交談時，漢娜打斷我們，說：「一起拍照吧。」

cut off

qiē chú

切除

The cook is cutting off the inedible parts of the vegetables.

廚師正在切除蔬菜中不能食用的部分。

cut out¹

<ruby>剪<rt>jiǎn</rt></ruby> <ruby>出<rt>chū</rt></ruby> <ruby>來<rt>lái</rt></ruby>

例句

The students are cutting out the shapes on the craft paper.

學生正在把手工紙上的圖案剪出來。

cut out²

jiè   chú
戒除

✨ 例句 ------------------------------

You should cut out junk food completely.

你應當徹底戒除垃圾食物。

date back

zhuī   sù
追溯

 例句 -

This church dates back to over 500 years.

這座教堂的歷史可追溯到500年前。

deal with

<ruby>應<rt>yìng</rt></ruby><ruby>對<rt>duì</rt></ruby>

100

 例句

She is an experienced nanny who is good at dealing with naughty kids.

她是一位很有經驗的保姆，擅長應對頑皮的小朋友。

depend on

xìn lài
信賴

 例句 -

Mr Chan is very capable. His boss depends on him to manage the office.

陳先生很能幹，老闆信賴他能管理好辦公室。

die out

jué zhǒng

絕種

 例句

It is believed that thylacines died out nearly 100 years ago.

據信袋狼在大約100年前絕種了。

dig in

kāi shǐ chī

開始吃

103

 例句 -

Dinner is ready. Let's dig in!

晚餐準備好了，大家開始吃吧！

dig out
wā chū
挖出

 例句

The puppy dug out a treasure box which was buried under the tree.

小狗挖出了埋在樹下的寶盒。

dine out

wài chū yòng shàn
外出用膳

例句

We usually dine out with our grandparents on Chinese New Year's Eve.

農曆除夕，我們通常會和祖父母外出用膳。

do over

chóng zuò
重做

Please redo it.

  例句 ----------------------------

I made too many mistakes in my homework. My teacher asked me to do it over.

我的功課犯了太多錯誤，老師要我重做一遍。

do up

kòu shàng　　niǔ kòu
扣上（鈕扣）

 例句 ----------

> do up 也可指「繫緊（鞋帶）」。

I could do up my coat when I was three years old.

我三歲時就懂得自己扣上外套的鈕扣。

doze off

shuì zháo
睡着

108

 例句

The children were so tired that they dozed off on the coach.

孩子們非常疲倦，在旅遊車上睡着了。

drag away

lā zǒu   mǒu rén
拉走（某人）

 例句

Mum dragged James away from the game booth.

媽媽把占士從遊戲攤位拉走。

drag into

<ruby>捲<rt>juǎn</rt></ruby><ruby>入<rt>rù</rt></ruby>

110

 例句 -

Kate was dragged into a disagreement between her colleagues.

凱蒂捲入了同事之間的分歧。

dream of

mèng xiǎng
夢想

111

 例句 - - - - - - - - - - - - - - -

He always dreams of opening a coffee shop at the seaside.

他一直夢想在海邊開設一間咖啡店。

dress up

zhuāng bàn
裝扮

✦ 例句 -

At the party, all the guests are required to dress up as animals.

在派對上，所有來賓都要裝扮成動物。

drift off

<ruby>漸<rt>jiàn</rt></ruby><ruby>漸<rt>jiàn</rt></ruby><ruby>入<rt>rù</rt></ruby><ruby>睡<rt>shuì</rt></ruby>

漸漸入睡

 例句 --------------------------------

The movie was so boring that I could not help drifting off.

電影太沉悶了，我不知不覺睡着了。

drink up

hē guāng
喝光

114

 例句 -

He was so thirsty that he drank up a bottle of water at once.

他太口渴了，一口氣喝光整瓶水。

drive off

jià chē lí kāi
駕車離開

 例句 --------------------------

Before driving off, drivers have to make sure there is nobody around.

司機駕車離開前，必須確保四周沒有人。

drop by

kàn wàng
看望

116

 例句 -

Aunt May dropped by our house after work.

美姨姨下班後來我們家看望我們。

drop out

tuì xué
退學

 例句 -

He dropped out of school because he decided to be a professional athlete.

他退學了，因為他決定成為職業運動員。

dry out

<ruby>乾<rt>gān</rt></ruby> <ruby>透<rt>tòu</rt></ruby>

 例句 ------------------------

The paint on the bench has not dried out yet.

長凳上的油漆還未乾透。

dry up

<ruby>擦<rt>cā</rt></ruby><ruby>乾<rt>gān</rt></ruby>

擦乾

119

 例句 -

Mum asked me to dry up the dishes before putting them in the cupboard.

媽媽吩咐我把餐具擦乾，才放進櫥櫃。

E

eat up

chī guāng
吃光

 例句 ----------------------------

He had a stomach ache because he had eaten up the whole bucket of ice cream.

他肚子痛，因為他把一整桶雪糕吃光了。

ice cream的普通話是「冰淇淋」。

end up

zuì zhōng biàn de
最終變得

例句

We meant to mop the floor but we ended up making a mess.

我們本來想拖地板，最終卻弄得一團糟。

face up to

zhèng shì
正視

122

 例句 -----------------------------

He has finally faced up to his obesity and started to have a healthy diet.

他終於正視自己的肥胖問題,開始健康飲食。

fall about

pěng fù dà xiào
捧腹大笑

 例句 -------------------

We fell about when we saw our little sister wearing our mum's shoes.

我們看見妹妹穿上媽媽的鞋子時，捧腹大笑起來。

fall down

<ruby>倒<rt>dǎo</rt></ruby><ruby>下<rt>xià</rt></ruby>

 例句 -

Many trees fell down after the typhoon.

颱風過後,很多樹木倒下了。

fall over

diē dǎo

跌倒

例句 ------------------------------------

Although he fell over, he did not cry.

雖然他跌倒了，但是他沒有哭。

feel for

tóng qíng
同情

 例句

Tommy has broken his leg and cannot play in the game. We really feel for him.

湯姆弄傷了腳，不能參加比賽，我們都很同情他。

figure out

<ruby>明<rt>míng</rt></ruby> <ruby>白<rt>bai</rt></ruby>

127

 例句 -

I cannot figure out the message of this painting.

我不明白這幅畫作想表達什麼。

fill in¹

tián xiě

填寫

例句

The candidate is filling in the job application form.

求職者正在填寫職位申請表格。

fill in²

dǐng tì
頂替

 例句 --------------------------

The receptionist is sick today. Therefore I need to fill in for her.

接待員今天生病了，所以我要頂替她。

fill up

tián mǎn
填滿

例句 -----------------------------

Amy filled the jar up with candies.
艾美用糖果裝滿了罐子。

find out

fā xiàn
發現

 例句

Mum found out that I had failed the test.

媽媽發現我測驗不及格。

fix up

xiū lǐ
修理

132

例句

Dad, the toy train is not working. Can you fix it up?

爸爸，玩具火車動不了，你可以修理它嗎？

focus on

jí zhōng

集中

 例句

This TV programme focuses on climate change.

這個電視節目集中討論氣候變化。

follow up

gēn jìn

跟進

例句

I found a wallet and gave it to the police. They would follow it up.

我拾到一個錢包,把它交給了警察。他們會跟進。

freak out

lìng rén jī dòng
令人激動

135

例句 --------------------------

Bobby was freaked out by the roar of the lion.

波比被獅子的吼叫聲嚇了一跳。

gear up

zhǔn bèi
準備

 例句 ----------------------------

The crew is gearing up for the voyage.

船員正在為航海旅程作準備。

get along

xiāng chǔ róng qià
相處融洽

137

例句 -

Our dogs get along with each other.

我們的狗相處融洽。

get back to

jì xù zuò mǒu shì
繼續做（某事）

 例句 -

We have taken enough rest. Let's get back to work.

我們休息夠了，繼續工作吧。

get down

lìng rén jǔ sàng
令人沮喪

 例句 - - - - - - - - - - - - - - - - - - -

Although he had already tried his best, the result of the exam got him down.

雖然他已經全力以赴了，但是考試成績令他很沮喪。

get into[1]

<ruby>參<rt>cān</rt></ruby><ruby>與<rt>yǔ</rt></ruby>

STUDENT UNION

 例句 ------------------------------

She got into the student union last year.

她由去年開始參與學生會事務。

get into²

huò qǔ lù
獲取錄

例句

She jumped for joy because she got into her dream ballet school.

她獲心儀的芭蕾舞學校取錄，非常高興。

get off[1]

xià bān

下班

 例句 -

Dad usually gets off at 5:30 p.m.

爸爸通常在下午五時三十分下班。

get off²

xià chē
下車

例句 --------------------------------

We have to get off at the next stop.

我們要在下一個站下車。

get out

lí kāi
離開

 例句 -

The rabbit is getting out of its burrow.

兔子正在離開洞穴。

get out of

táo bì
逃避

 例句 ----------------------------

She is afraid of water so she wants to get out of the swimming class.

她很怕水，所以她想逃避上游泳課。

get over

huī fù guò lái
恢復過來

146

 例句 ---------------------------

You need to take more rest to get over the sickness.

你要多休息，才能康復過來。

get through

tōng guò

通過

例句 - - - - -

get through 多指通過測驗、考試。

She got through the driving test easily.

她輕易通過了駕駛考試。

get up

qǐ chuáng

起牀

 例句 -

We have to get up at 6:30 a.m. on school days.

上學的日子，我們要在早上六時三十分起牀。

give away

sòng chū
送出

149

 例句 ----------------------------

The game booth gives away colourful balloons to attract children.

遊戲攤位送出色彩繽紛的氣球，吸引小朋友前來。

give back

guī　huán
歸還

150

This is my robot. Give it back to me!

這是我的機械人，還給我！

G

give in

ràng bù
讓步

151

 例句 ------------------------

Stop crying! You have many toys at home.
I am not giving in this time.

不要哭了！你已經有很多玩具在家裏，這次我
不會讓步。

give up

fàng qì
放棄

 例句

I have given up the book because it is too boring.

我放棄了閱讀這本書，因為它太沉悶了。

G

go ahead

kāi shǐ zuò mǒu shì

開始做（某事）

153

 例句 -

Miss Chan has approved our decoration design for the classroom. Let's go ahead.

陳老師批准了我們裝飾教室的設計，我們開始布置吧。

go away

<ruby>走<rt>zǒu</rt></ruby><ruby>開<rt>kāi</rt></ruby>

154

例句 -------------------------

Jenny saw a mouse and screamed at it, "Go away!"

珍妮看見老鼠，尖叫起來：「走開！」

go back

fǎn huí
返回

155

 例句 --------------------------

We go back to our classroom after recess.

小息後，我們返回教室。

go for

xuǎn zé
選擇

例句 -

Um, I think I will go for the comedy.

嗯，我想我會選擇看喜劇。

go in for

xǐ huan
喜歡

 例句 -

Aunt Sophie has gone in for gardening ever since she moved to the countryside.

蘇菲姨姨自從搬到鄉村後，就喜歡上園藝。

go off

biàn huài
變壞

 例句 - - - -

go off 多指食物、飲料變壞。

Yuck! The milk tastes sour. I think it has gone off.

真噁心！牛奶很酸，我想是變壞了。

go on

fā shēng
發生

What is going on here?

例句

What is going on here?
這裏發生什麼事？

go out

_{wài} _{chū}
外出

160

 例句 -

Don't forget to lock the door when you go out.

出門時，別忘了鎖門。

go over

wēn xí
溫習

 例句 --------------------------------

We have formed a study group to go over our textbooks regularly.

我們成立了學習小組，定期溫習課本。

go through

zǐ xì jiǎn chá
仔細檢查

162

例句 -

The detective is going through all the drawers at the crime scene.

偵探正在仔細檢查案發現場的所有抽屜。

go up to

tōng wǎng

通往

 例句 ----------------------------

The footpath goes up to the top of the hill.

這條小徑一直通往山頂。

go with

xiāng pèi
相配

 例句 -----------------------------

Caramel goes very well with vanilla ice cream.

焦糖和雲呢拿雪糕非常相配。

vanilla 的普通話是「香草」；ice cream 的普通話是「冰淇淋」。

grow apart

zhú jiàn shū yuǎn
逐漸疏遠

 例句 -

Vicki and I have grown apart after we graduated.

維琪和我畢業後，就逐漸疏遠了。

grow into

zhǎng dà hòu biàn chéng

長大後變成

2014 2023

He used to be a chubby boy. He has now grown into a handsome tall man.

他從前是一個胖乎乎的男孩。現在長大後，他變得又高又英俊。

grow up

zhǎng dà
長大

例句

I want to be a pilot when I grow up.

長大後，我想成為飛機師。

hand in

tí jiāo

提交

168

例句

- -

She managed to hand in her assignment to the professor on time.

她順利準時提交功課給教授。

hang back

yóu yù
猶豫

例句

He hung back at the poolside, feeling scared to dive in.

他在泳池邊猶豫起來，害怕跳入水中。

hang onto

bǎo liú
保留

 例句 -

Hang onto the magazine. I have not read it yet.

請保留這本雜誌，我還未看呢。

hang out

xiāo mó shí jiān
消磨時間

171

 例句 --------------------------------

At weekends, she usually hangs out with her friends at shopping malls.

周末，她常常和朋友在購物商場消磨時間。

hang up

guà duàn diàn huà
掛斷電話

 例句 ----------------------------

My boss is coming. I have to hang up now.
老闆來了，我要掛斷電話了。

hear out

tīng　　mǒu rén　　shuō wán
聽（某人）說完

173

 例句 -

Please hear me out first. I will let you ask your question later.

請先聽我說完，我稍後會讓你發問。

heat up

_{jiā rè}
加熱

 例句 -

It takes less than a minute to heat up a chicken pie in a microwave oven.

用微波爐加熱雞肉餡餅，只需不到一分鐘的
時間。

help out

bāng máng

幫忙

Can you help me out?

 例句

The suitcase is too heavy. Can you help me out?

行李箱太重了，你可以幫我嗎？

hold back

tuì suō
退縮

176

 例句 -

The thief held back immediately when he saw a policeman coming.

賊人看見警察時，立刻退縮了。

hold on

_{děng yí xià}

等一下

177

 例句 --------------------------

Hold on! I am still wearing my shoes.

等一下！我還在穿鞋子。

hold up¹

dān wu
耽誤

例句 -----------------------------

The flights were held up due to the typhoon.

受颱風吹襲影響，航班延誤了。

hold up²

zhī chēng
支撐

例句 -

The tent is held up by a few poles.

帳篷由幾枝桿子支撐着。

hurry up

gǎn kuài
趕快

 例句 ----------------------------

Hurry up or we will be late for school.

趕快點，否則我們上學會遲到。

jot down

kuài sù jì xià
快速記下

 例句 --------------------------------

The secretary is jotting down what her boss asks her to do.

秘書正在快速記下老闆吩咐她做的事。

jump out at

xī yǐn zhù yì

吸引注意

 例句

This dress looks very special. It really jumps out at me.

這條裙子很特別，我一下子就注意到它。

keep off

yuǎn lí
遠離

183

 例句 --------------------------

You must keep off the grass in the park.

請勿踐踏公園裏的草地。

keep on

bù tíng zuò mǒu shì
不停做（某事）

184

 例句

The girl kept on asking her mum to buy her the doll.

女孩不停請求媽媽給她買那個洋娃娃。

keep up with

zhuī shàng
追上

 例句 ------------------------------

Slow down! I cannot keep up with you.

慢下來！我追不上你。

key in

shū rù
輸入

 例句 ------------------------------

Residents need to key in the password to enter the building.

住客需要輸入密碼，才能進入大廈。

kick off

kāi shǐ

開始

例句

As soon as the starting pistol fired, the marathon kicked off.

發令槍一響，馬拉松就開始了。

kick out

kāi　chú
開除

 例句 -

He got kicked out of the track and field team because he is too slow.

他被田徑隊除名了，因為他跑得太慢。

knock down

zhuàng dǎo

撞倒

 例句 -

The dog was knocked down by a car.

狗被車撞倒了。

knock up

qiāo mén huàn xǐng
敲門喚醒

190

 例句 -

It is time to go to school. Mum is knocking Danny up.

是時候上學了。媽媽正在敲門喚醒丹尼。

laugh at

qǔ xiào
取笑

 例句 - - - - - - - - - - - - - - - - - - -

Everybody is laughing at him because he forgot to wear his shoes.

所有人都在取笑他，因為他忘記了穿鞋子。

lay off

jiě gù
解僱

192

 例句 --------------------------------

Due to the economic downturn, a few shop assistants were laid off.

由於經濟不景，幾位店員被解僱了。

lay on

tí gōng

提供

 例句 -

Light refreshments will be laid on after the activity.

活動結束後，將會提供簡單茶點。

lay out

bǎi　fàng
擺放

194

 例句 ------------------------------

The stallholder laid out the fresh vegetables.

檔主把新鮮的蔬菜擺放出來了。

lead to

dǎo zhì
導致

 例句 -

Heavy rainfall can lead to severe flooding.

大雨可導致嚴重水浸。

leave behind

yí   lòu
遺漏

Anna has left behind her homework at home.

安娜把功課遺漏在家。

leave to

liú gěi mǒu rén chǔ lǐ
留給（某人）處理

例句 ----------------------------

The bucket is too heavy. Leave it to me.
水桶太重了，留給我來拿吧。

L

let in

yǔn xǔ jìn rù
允許進入

198

例句 -----------------------------

We should never let a stranger in.

我們不應允許陌生人進來。

let off

cóng qīng chǔ fá
從輕處罰

 例句

Mr Lau knew I had broken the glass window by accident so he let me off.

劉老師知道我不是故意打破玻璃窗，所以他從輕發落。

lie around

luàn fàng
亂放

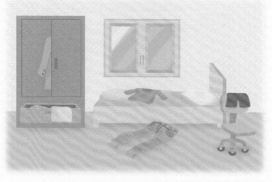

 例句 -

Do not leave your clothes lying around.

不要亂放衣服。

lie back

xiàng hòu tǎng
向後躺

 例句 -

We lay back in the deckchairs to enjoy the beautiful sunset.

我們向後躺在沙灘椅上，欣賞美麗的日落。

lie down

tǎng xià
躺下

202

 例句 ----------------------------

We lay down on the grass, watching the white clouds scudding across the sky.

我們在草地上躺下來，觀看天上掠過的白雲。

lie in

shuì lǎn jiào
睡懶覺

 例句

It was my day off yesterday so I could lie in until noon.

昨天我休假，所以我可以睡懶覺直到中午。

light up

xiǎn de gāo xìng

顯得高興

 例句

The children's faces light up when they see the clown.

孩子們看見小丑時，都顯得很高興。

lighten up

fàng sōng
放鬆

例句

The English teacher played a game with us to lighten up the lesson.

英文老師和我們玩了一個遊戲，讓課堂氣氛輕鬆起來。

line up

pái duì

排隊

206

 例句 --------------------------------

In school assembly, the students line up in order of height.

在學校集會上，學生按身高排隊。

listen in on

tōu tīng
偷聽

 例句

The secret agent is listening in on a telephone conversation.

秘密特工正在竊聽一通電話。

listen up
liú xīn tīng
留心聽

208

 例句 -

"Listen up, everybody! We are going to take a rest here!" the leader called.

隊長高聲說：「各位，請注意！我們會在這裏休息一下！」

ENG × 粵語

ENG × 普通話

live for

wéi　　mǒu shì　　ér huó
為（某事）而活

209

 例句 -

He is a singer who lives for music.

他是一位為音樂而活的歌手。

load up on

dà liàng gòu mǎi
大量購買

210

例句

People are loading up on food as the snowstorm is coming.

快要颳暴風雪了，人們趕着大量購買食物。

look after

zhào gù
照顧

211

 例句 --------------------------------

When my parents go to work, my grandparents look after me.

父母外出工作時，祖父母會照顧我。

look down on

kàn bu qǐ

看不起

212

 例句

He is so arrogant that he looks down on people who are not as smart as him.

他很傲慢，看不起不及他聰明的人。

look for

xún zhǎo

尋找

213

 例句 ----------------------------

Grandma is looking for her glasses.

祖母正在尋找她的眼鏡。

look forward to

qī dài

期待

214

 例句 -

She is looking forward to the school picnic tomorrow.

她期待明天的學校旅行。

look into

_{yán} _{jiū}
研究

 例句

The repairman is looking into the water leakage in our bathroom.

維修工人正在研究我們浴室內的滲水情況。

look on

shì wéi
視為

216

 例句

The couple look on their cat as their own child.

這對夫婦把他們的貓視為自己的孩子。

look through

kuài sù yuè lǎn
快速閱覽

 例句 -

Dad is looking through the menu to see what dishes to order.

爸爸正在快速閱覽菜單，看看要點什麼菜。

look up

_{chá} _{yuè}
查閱

218

 例句 -

I don't know how to bake a cake. Let me look up the recipe.

我不懂得焗蛋糕，讓我查閱一下食譜吧。

look up to

jìng zhòng
敬重

 例句 --------------------------

Our principal is very wise and knowledgeable. We all look up to him.

校長很有智慧和學識，我們都很敬重他。

make up¹

xū gòu
虛構

 例句

He is not sick. He just made that up to get rid of the housework.

他沒有生病,他只是編造藉口來逃避做家務。

make up²

hé jiě
和解

例句 ----------------------------

They hugged each other and made up after an argument.

爭吵過後，他們擁抱彼此，和好如初。

make up³

huà zhuāng
化妝

  例句 -

The teachers are making the children up as animals.

老師正在為小朋友化妝，把他們裝扮成動物。

make up for

<ruby>彌<rt>mí</rt></ruby><ruby>補<rt>bǔ</rt></ruby>

Sorry!

223

例句

Terry had broken my robot so he bought me a new one to make up for it.

泰利弄壞了我的機械人，所以他買了一個新的給我作補償。

meet up

<ruby>相<rt>xiāng</rt>聚<rt>jù</rt></ruby>

 例句

My best friend and I meet up for dinner once a week.

我和我最好的朋友每星期都會相聚一次吃晚飯。

mess around

hú nào
胡鬧

225

 例句 -

Don't mess around with the umbrella.

不要亂玩雨傘。

mess up

nòng luàn
弄亂

 例句 -

The children messed up the kitchen.

孩子們把廚房弄得亂七八糟。

miss out

cuò guò
錯過

 例句

What a shame! I have missed out on the good deal.

真可惜！我錯過了撿便宜的好機會。

mix up

hùn　xiáo

混淆

sugar　salt

228

 例句

The cake tastes terrible — I got salt and sugar mixed up.

蛋糕很難吃——我把鹽和糖混淆了。

mop up

yòng tuō bǎ mā qián
用拖把抹乾

 例句 -----------------------------

It is okay! Let me mop it up.

不要緊，讓我用拖把抹乾。

move out

bān zǒu
搬走

230

 例句 -

My elder sister will move out after her wedding.

姊姊結婚後就會搬走。

order in

jiào wài mài
叫外賣

231

 例句 -----------------------------

I did not have time to cook so I ordered in a pizza for dinner.

我沒有時間煮食，所以叫了外賣，吃薄餅做晚餐。

pass around

fēn　fā
分發

232

 例句 -------------------------------

The monitor is passing the workbooks around.

班長正在分發作業。

pass away

lí shi
離世

 例句 ----------------------------

My grandmother passed away peacefully in her sleep last week.

上星期，祖母在睡夢中安詳離世。

pass down

chuán gěi hòu rén

傳給後人

2020 | 2060

 例句

Grandma passed this bracelet down to mum; mum will pass it down to me.

祖母把這隻手鐲傳給了媽媽；媽媽將來會把它傳給我。

pass on

gào su
告訴

 例句 -

The meeting is cancelled. Please pass it on to the colleagues.

會議取消了，請告訴同事。

pass out

shī qù zhī jué
失去知覺

236

 例句 ----------------------------

He passed out after being hit by a tennis ball.

他被網球擊中，失去了知覺。

P

ENG × 粵語

ENG × 普通話

pay back

cháng huán

償還

237

 例句 ----------------------------

How much did you pay for my lunch yesterday? Let me pay you back.

昨天的午餐，你替我付了多少錢？我要還給你。

pay for

fù chū dài jià
付出代價

 例句

You have to pay for eating too many sweets.

你吃太多糖果了，要付出代價。

pick at

tiǎo nòng shí wù
挑弄食物

239

例句 --------------------------

Why are you picking at your food? Do you not like noodles?

你為什麼在挑弄食物？你不喜歡吃麵條嗎？

pick on

diāo　nàn
刁難

240

例句 -----------------------

This difficult customer picked on the new waitress.

這個難纏的顧客刁難了新來的女侍應生。

pick up¹

jiē huí
接回

 例句 ------------------

My grandpa picks me up after school every day.

祖父每天都接我放學。

pick up²

xué huì
學會

242

The new salesman has picked things up quickly.

新來的售貨員很快就上手了。

pick up³

shí qǐ
拾起

 例句

She picked up a beautiful shell on the beach.

她在沙灘拾起了一個漂亮的貝殼。

play at

jiǎ　bàn
假扮

244

 例句

When we were little, we always played at being superheroes.

小時候，我們經常假扮成超級英雄。

plug in

jiē tōng diàn yuán
接通電源

例句

We cheered as the Christmas lights got plugged in.

聖誕燈飾亮起一刻,我們歡呼起來。

point out

zhǐ chū
指出

例句

Mr Chan pointed out the typo on the poster.

陳老師指出了海報上的錯字。

ENG × 粵語

ENG × 普通話

pour out

_{qīng} _{sù}
傾訴

例句 ----------------------------

She is pouring out her stress of the job to her colleague.

她正在向同事傾訴她的工作壓力。

pull at

qīng qīng lā chě
輕輕拉扯

例句

Helen is pulling at my sleeve, reminding me to pay attention.

海倫輕輕拉扯我的衣袖，提醒我要留心。

pull on

gǎn kuài chuān dài
趕快穿戴

 例句 ----------------------------

We are being late! Just pull something on!
我們要遲到了！趕快穿上衣服！

push in

chā duì

插隊

250

例句

People glared at the man who had pushed in.

人們怒目瞪視那個插隊的男人。

put across

qīng chu biǎo dá
清楚表達

 例句 -----------------------------

She does not like outdoor activities.
She puts across it well.

她不喜歡戶外活動，她清楚表達了出來。

put away

shōu qǐ
收起

 例句 ------------------------------

Please put away your books.

請收起書本。

ENG × 粵語

ENG × 普通話

put back

fàng huí yuán chù
放回原處

253

例句

Please put the shopping basket back in its place after use.

使用後請把購物籃放回原處。

put down[1]

xiě xià
寫下

 例句

The teacher asked the students to put down their names on the exam paper.

老師叫學生在試卷上寫下自己的名字。

P

put down²

fàng xià
放下

 例句 ----------------------------

We put down our backpacks and took a rest.

我們放下背包，休息了一會。

put off[1]

yán hòu
延後

WED	THU	FRI	SAT
1	2	3	4
8	9	10	11
15	16	17	18

 例句

Tommy is not feeling well. We have to put off the picnic.

湯姆身體不適，我們要推遲野餐。

P

put off²

lìng rén fǎn gǎn
令人反感

257

例句

The fishy smell from the stall really puts me off.

攤檔的魚腥味真的令我很反感。

put on

chuān shàng

穿上

258

 例句 -

He is putting on his thick down jacket.

他正在穿上厚羽絨外套。

put onto

jiè shào
介紹

Thank you.

例句 ----------------------------

Thank you for putting me onto this amazing novel.

謝謝你向我介紹這本精彩的小說。

put out

xī　miè
熄滅

 例句 -

We should put out the fire in the pit before we leave.

離開前，我們要熄滅燒烤爐的火。

put together

pīn còu
拼湊

 例句 -

Andy made a robot by putting the cans together.

安迪用罐子拼湊出一個機械人。

put up

zhāng tiē
張貼

262

 例句 ----------------------------

The shop assistant is putting up a promotional poster.

店員正在張貼宣傳海報。

put up with

rěn shòu
忍受

 例句 ----------------------------

I can't put up with my elder brother's snores so I put in the earplugs.

我忍受不了哥哥的鼻鼾聲，所以我佩戴耳塞。

rat on

chū mài
出賣

264

✨ 例句 ━━━━━━━━━━━━━━━━━━━━━━

The gangster rat on his partners and told the police where they were hiding.

歹徒出賣同黨，告訴警察他們躲藏在哪裏。

reach out

shēn chū yuán shǒu
伸出援手

例句 --------------------

The volunteers reached out to the underprivileged.

義工們向弱勢社羣伸出援手。

read out

<ruby>朗<rt>lǎng</rt></ruby><ruby>讀<rt>dú</rt></ruby>

例句

Miss Wong asked me to read out the text in front of the class.

黃老師請我在同學面前朗讀課文。

read through

kuài sù yuè dú
快速閱讀

 例句

After reading through the play, the director decided to turn it into a movie.

導演快速讀遍劇本後，決定把它拍成電影。

result from

<small>yóu yú</small>
由於

268

 例句

Her tanned skin results from her passion for water sports.

她一身黝黑的膚色，是源於她對水上運動的熱愛。

roll back

^{jiǎn} ^{jià}
減價

 例句 ------------------------

No one would buy a chair at such a high price. Roll it back.

沒有人會買這麼昂貴的椅子，減價吧。

roll out

tuī chū
推出

270

例句

roll out 多指推出新產品、服務等。

Our shop has rolled out a new series of bedding sets.

本店推出了一系列全新的牀上用品套裝。

run after

zhuī zhú

追逐

271

 例句 ----------------------------

The little cat is running after the mouse.

小貓正在追逐老鼠。

run around

máng　lù
忙碌

 例句 -

Mum has been running around all day preparing for dinner.

媽媽為了準備晚餐，忙碌了一整天。

run away

tǎo zǒu
逃走

 例句 ----------------------------

He has stolen my wallet. Don't let him run away.

他偷了我的錢包，不要讓他逃走。

run into

ǒu yù
偶遇

 例句 -

I ran into my friend in the museum last week.

上星期，我在博物館偶遇了我的朋友。

run out

yòng wán
用完

 例句 ----------------------------

Mum, we have run out of toilet paper.

媽媽，衞生紙用完了。

save on

jié shěng

節省

 例句 -

Bringing a lunch box is a good way to save on expenses.

自備午餐是節省開支的好方法。

save up

<ruby>儲<rt>chǔ</rt>蓄<rt>xù</rt></ruby>

例句 -

Andy is saving up for a new watch.

安迪正在儲蓄，想買一隻新手錶。

scare into

xié pò
脅迫

 例句 ------------------------

The bully is scaring the little boy into giving up the swing.

惡霸正在脅迫小男孩讓出鞦韆。

✎ swing 的普通話是「鞦韆」。

scare off

xià pǎo
嚇跑

 例句 -

The little girl was scared off by the lifelike stuffed animal.

小女孩被逼真的動物布偶嚇跑了。

see off

sòng bié
送別

DEPARTURES

280

例句

Ray is going to study abroad. We are seeing him off at the airport.

小雷即將出國留學，我們在機場送別他。

send out

jì chū
寄出

 例句

Every year, we send out many Christmas cards to our relatives and friends.

每年，我們都寄出很多聖誕卡給親友。

set down

ràng chéng kè xià chē
讓乘客下車

 例句

The school bus set the students down at the entrance of the school.

校車停在學校門口，讓學生下車。

set off

^{chū} ^{fā}
出發

 例句 -

They packed their backpacks and set off
for a short trip.

他們收拾背包，出發去短途旅行。

set up

shè lì

設立

 例句

A recycling station is set up in our neighbourhood.

我們的社區設立了一個回收站。

settle down

shì yìng
適應

例句 - - - - -

settle down 多指適應新環境。

We are settling down quite well in this new neighbourhood.

我們在新社區適應得不錯。

settle for

wú nài jiē shòu
無奈接受

286

 例句

She did not have enough money for a layer cake so she settled for a basic one.

她不夠錢買千層蛋糕，只好購買款式簡單的蛋糕。

shop around

huò bǐ sān jiā
貨比三家

例句

After shopping around, she decided to buy the washing machine in this shop.

她比較過幾間商店後，決定在這間店鋪購買洗衣機。

show around

dài lǐng cān guān
帶領參觀

 例句 -

The zookeeper is showing the children around the zoo.

動物園管理員正在帶領小朋友參觀動物園。

show off

xuàn yào
炫耀

 例句 -

She is showing off her sparkling diamond engagement ring to her friends.

她正在向朋友們炫耀閃爍的鑽石訂婚戒指。

show up

lòu miàn
露面

 例句 -

After all the guests had arrived, the birthday girl finally showed up.

所有賓客到達後，壽星女終於露面了。

shut off

fēng bì
封閉

291

例句

After her cat got lost, she has shut herself off and refused to see anyone.

她的貓走失後，她把自己封閉起來，拒絕見任何人。

shut up

bì zuǐ
閉嘴

 例句 ----------------------------

The students shut themselves up as soon as the teacher came in.

老師一進來，學生就閉上嘴巴了。

sign up

bào míng cān jiū
報名參加

 例句 -

We have signed up for the basketball class.

我們報名參加了籃球班。

sit back[1]

xiàng hòu kào zhe zuò
向後靠着坐

  例句 -------------------------------

Mum, sit back and relax. I have made you some tea.

媽媽，坐下來放鬆一下。我泡了茶給你。

sit back²

zuò shì bù lǐ
坐視不理

 例句 -----------------------

While we were busy doing the group project, he was just sitting back.

當我們正忙於做小組專題研習時,他坐着什麼都不理。

sit down

zuò xià
坐下

 例句 -

You may sit down now.

你們可以坐下了。

sit up

zuò zhí
坐直

297

 例句 -

Miss Chan reminded me to sit up straight.

陳老師提醒我要坐直身子。

slow down

fàng màn
放慢

  例句

Drivers should slow down when the road is wet.

道路濕滑時，司機應減慢車速。

sort out

jiǎn xuǎn chū
揀選出

299

 例句 --------------------------

The children are sorting out recyclable materials.

小朋友正在揀選出可回收重用的物料。

speak up

shuō dà shēng diǎn
說大聲點

300

 例句

If you want to be heard, you need to speak up a little.

如果想別人聽到你說話，你就要稍微說大
聲點。

speed up

jiā kuài
加快

301

 例句 ----------------------------

We need many more workers to speed up the construction.

我們需要更多工人，以加快工程進度。

spice up

zēng tiān qù wèi
增添趣味

302

 例句 ------------------------------

Some interactive games are added to spice up the drama.

戲劇加入了一些互動遊戲，以增添趣味。

spill out¹

diào chu
掉出

例句 -

The popcorn is spilling out of the bucket.

爆谷從桶裏掉出來。

popcorn的普通話是「玉米花」。

spill out²

rén qún yǒng chū
人羣湧出

304

 例句

Commuters are spilling out of the train onto the platform.

上班族從列車湧出到月台上。

spread out

sàn kāi
散開

 例句 ------------------------------

The volunteers spread out to pick up rubbish in the country park.

義工在郊野公園分頭撿垃圾。

stand back

tuì hòu
退後

 例句 -

The policemen asked the bystanders to stand back and leave the accident scene.

警察呼籲圍觀者退後，離開意外現場。

stand by[1]

zhī chí
支持

 例句 ------------------------

A good friend always stands by you.
好朋友會一直支持你。

stand by²

zuò hǎo zhǔn bèi
做好準備

 例句

A few first-aiders are standing by in case any runners need help.

幾位急救員做好準備，以防任何跑手需要幫助。

stand out

tū chū
突出

309

 例句 ----------------------------

Her fancy hat makes her stand out in the crowd.

她那頂花俏的帽子，讓她突出在人羣中。

stand up¹

zhàn lì
站立

 例句

Peter stood up and answered the teacher's question.

彼得站了起來，回答老師的問題。

stand up²

shī yuē
失約

 例句 --------------------------------

After waiting for an hour, he realised that he had got stood up.

他等了一個小時後，才意識到自己被爽約了。

start out

kāi shǐ
開始

312

✦ 例句

start out 多指開始
職業生涯。

The owner of the restaurant started out as a kitchen assistant.

餐廳的東主最初是一名廚房助理。

start up

chéng lì
成立

313

 例句

Mike started up a software company after his graduation.

米克畢業後，成立了一間電腦軟件公司。

stay away from

yuǎn   lí
遠離

 例句

During the typhoon, we should stay away from the coast.

颱風吹襲期間，我們應該遠離岸邊。

stay behind

liú xià bù zǒu
留下不走

315

 例句 -

After the graduation ceremony, the graduates stayed behind and took photos with their families.

畢業典禮完結後，畢業生留下來和家人拍照。

stay in

liú zài jiā zhōng
留在家中

 例句 -

After a week of hard work, he prefers to stay in and relax.

經過一周的辛勤工作，他選擇留在家中放鬆。

stay out of

zhì shen shì wài

置身事外

 例句 ------------------------------

When we have an argument, our dad always stays out of it.

當我們吵架時，爸爸總是不介入其中。

stay over

zài wài liú sù

在外留宿

318

 例句 ----------------------------

He is very excited to stay over at his friend's home tonight.

他很興奮今晚在朋友家中留宿。

stay up

shēn yè wèi mián

深夜未眠

 例句 -

They stayed up to watch the football match last night.

昨晚他們熬夜觀看足球比賽。

S

319

step aside

ràng kāi
讓開

Step aside, please!

例句

"Step aside, please!" the nurse said while pushing the patient in the wheelchair.

護士一邊推着輪椅上的病人，一邊說：「請讓開。」

step down

<ruby>退<rt>tuì</rt></ruby><ruby>位<rt>wèi</rt></ruby>

 例句 -

Our principal has decided to step down and retire next year.

我們的校長決定明年辭職退休。

stick at

jiān chí zuò mǒu shì
堅持做（某事）

322

 例句 -----------------------------

Despite the long working hours, he still sticks at the job.

雖然工作時間很長，但是他仍然緊守崗位。

stick out

<ruby>露<rt>lù</rt></ruby><ruby>出<rt>chū</rt></ruby>

 例句 -------------------

A cleaning cloth was sticking out of the cupboard.

櫥櫃露出了一塊清潔抹布。

swing around

kuài sù zhuǎn shēn
快速轉身

324

I swung around to see who was tapping me on my shoulder.

我快速轉身去看是誰拍我的肩膀。

take after

xiūng xiàng
相像

325

 例句 -

Many people say I take after my father.

很多人說我長得像爸爸。

take away

_{ná zǒu}
拿走

Take away the boxes! They are blocking the door.

拿走這些箱子！它們堵住了門口。

take off[1]

tuō xià
脫下

327

 例句

When you go into a church, you should take off your sunglasses.

進入教堂時，要摘下太陽眼鏡。

take off²

qǐ fēi
起飛

 例句 --------------------------------

The boys are excited to see a plane taking off.

男孩們很興奮看見飛機起飛。

take off³

xiū jià
休假

 例句

Mary took a day off to go hiking with friends.

瑪莉休假一天，和朋友去遠足。

take out

dài mǒu rén chū qù
帶（某人）出去

330

 例句

My grandparents took us out to the park.

祖父母帶我們去公園。

take up

zhàn jù
佔據

 例句 - - - - - - -

> take up 多指佔據時間或地方。

This vase takes up too much space.

這個花瓶太佔地方了。

T

ENG × 粵語

ENG × 普通話

talk into

shuō fú
說服

332

 例句

Cindy was too shy, but we talked her into dancing with us.

仙迪太害羞了，但是我們說服了她一起去跳舞。

talk over

tǎo lùn
討論

 例句 -

The group is talking over the arrangement for the camping.

組員正在討論露營的安排。

tear apart

sī kāi
撕開

 例句

My baby brother tore apart my workbook.
小弟弟把我的作業撕破了。

tear up

<ruby>含<rt>hán</rt></ruby><ruby>淚<rt>lèi</rt></ruby>
含淚

 例句 -

She tore up as she saw her mum leaving.

她看見媽媽離開時，雙眼充滿了淚水。

ENG × 粵語

ENG × 普通話

tell off

zé bèi
責備

336

 例句

Mum told me off for tossing the ball and breaking the vase.

媽媽責備我亂拋皮球，把花瓶打破了。

tell on

gào fā
告發

 例句 -

My little brother told my mother on me
because I had broken the mug.

弟弟向媽媽告發我，因為我打破了杯子。

think about

xiǎng qǐ
想起

338

 例句

I always think about Christmas when I eat gingerbread cookies.

當我吃薑餅時，總是會想起聖誕節。

think back

huí xiǎng
回想

例句 ------

Dad thought back to his childhood when he saw the spinning top.

爸爸看見陀螺時，回想起他的童年時光。

think of

<ruby>想<rt>xiǎng</rt></ruby><ruby>出<rt>chū</rt></ruby>

想出

340

例句

Benny thought of a smart way to keep his puppy dry in the rain.

賓尼想出了一個聰明的方法，讓小狗在雨中保持乾爽。

think over

rèn zhēn kǎo lù
認真考慮

 例句 ----------------------------

Buying a car is a big decision. I need to think it over.

買車是一個重大決定,我需要認真考慮。

throw away

diū qì
丟棄

 例句 - - - - - - - - - - - - - - - - - - -

The bread is mouldy. Throw it away!

麵包發黴了，丟棄它吧！

throw into

tóu rù yú

投入於

 例句

Ever since the couple retired, they have thrown themselves into voluntary work.

這對夫婦自退休後，就全情投入參與義工服務。

ENG × 粵語

ENG × 普通話

throw up

ǒu tù
嘔吐

344

例句

I got airsick. I had been throwing up on the plane.

我暈機了，在飛機上不停嘔吐。

tie up

kǔn zā

捆紮

例句

I tied the gift up with a golden ribbon.

我用一條金色絲帶把禮物捆起來。

tip over

fān dǎo
翻倒

 例句

He accidentally tipped over his bowl.

他不小心打翻了自己的碗。

top up¹

^{tiān jiā}
添加

 例句 -

May I top up your coffee, sir?

先生，給你添些咖啡好嗎？

top up²

zēng zhí
增值

例句

You can top up your travel card in any convenience stores.

你可以在任何一間便利店增值交通卡。

trip up

bàn dǎo
絆倒

 例句 ----------------------------

He tripped up on the rocky path.

他在崎嶇的小徑上絆倒了。

try on

_{shì chuān} _{shì dài}
試穿；試戴

 例句

She is trying on some hats. She cannot decide which one to buy.

她正在試戴幾頂帽子。她決定不了要買哪一頂。

try out

cè shì
測試

 例句 -

The salesman says this remote-controlled car can go very fast. Let's try it out!

售貨員說這輛遙控車可以開得很快。我們來試試看吧！

ENG × 粵語

ENG × 普通話

tuck in

wéi hái zi gài bèi zi

（為孩子）蓋被子

352

 例句

> tuck in 可延伸指「哄孩子睡覺」。

The baby falls asleep quickly whenever his mum tucks him in.

每當媽媽為這個嬰兒蓋好被子，他就會很快入睡。

turn away

zhuǎn guò liǎn qù

轉過臉去

 例句

The movie was too frightening that I turned away almost the whole time.

電影太恐怖了，我幾乎一直轉過臉去。

turn down[1]

tiáo dī
調低

 例句 -

The baby is sleeping. Please turn down the volume.

嬰兒正在睡覺，請調低音量。

turn down²

jù   jué

拒絕

355

 例句 -

Tom invited Bella for dinner but she
turned him down.

湯姆邀請貝拉共晉晚餐，但是她拒絕了。

turn into

biàn chéng
變成

 例句 -

Sally is very creative. She has turned a
pair of old jeans into a shopping bag.

莎莉很有創意。她改造了一條舊牛仔褲，
把它變成購物袋。

T

turn off

_{guān} _{diào}
關掉

357

 例句 -

Remember to turn off the light before you leave.

離開前記得關燈。

turn on

<ruby>開<rt>kāi</rt></ruby><ruby>啟<rt>qǐ</rt></ruby>

358

 例句 ------------------------------

It is hot. Turn on the fan, please.

天氣很熱，請開啟電風扇。

turn to

qiú zhù yú
求助於

 例句 -

Whenever I get into trouble, I turn to my grandma.

每當我遇到麻煩，都會向祖母求助。

turn up

_{tiáo} _{gāo}
調高

例句

I cannot hear the music. Would you please turn it up?

我聽不到音樂,請問可以把音量調高嗎?

use up

yòng guāng
用光

 例句 ------------------------------

The ketchup is used up.

茄汁用光了。

wait for

děng dài
等待

  例句 -

I have been waiting for you for an hour.

我已經等了你一個小時。

wait on

ci　hou
伺候

 例句 ----------------------------

He quit his job to wait on his sick father.

他辭掉了工作，伺候生病的爸爸。

wait up

bú　shuì　jiào
不睡覺

364

 例句 - - - - -

wait up 多用於等某人回家。

Dad will be home very late tonight but I will wait up for him.

爸爸今晚會很晚才回家，但是我會等他。

walk away

yì zǒu liǎo zhī
一走了之

 例句 --------------------------------

I saw the boy litter and walk away.

我看見那個男孩亂拋垃圾，然後一走了之。

walk through

xiáng xì jiě shì

詳細解釋

 例句

Peter is walking grandpa through how to use the computer.

彼得正在向祖父詳細解釋如何使用電腦。

ward off

bì kāi
避開

367

 例句 --------------------------------

She is waving her hands to ward off the mosquitoes.

她正在揮動雙手，驅走蚊子。

warm up

rè shēn

熱身

368

✦ 例句 ----------------------------

It is important to warm up before you do exercise.

運動前熱身是很重要的。

wash off

<ruby>洗<rt>xǐ</rt></ruby><ruby>掉<rt>diào</rt></ruby>

洗掉

  例句 --------------------------

I am washing the sand off.

我正在洗掉沙子。

wash up

xǐ wǎn dié

洗碗碟

370

 例句 ----------------------------

It is my turn to wash up the dishes tonight.

今晚輪到我洗碗碟。

watch out

<ruby>當<rt>dāng</rt></ruby><ruby>心<rt>xīn</rt></ruby>

 例句

Watch out! The teapot is very hot!

當心！茶壺很燙手！

371

wind up

lìng rén shēng qì
令人生氣

 例句

My little brother always pulls my hair and it really winds me up.

弟弟經常扯我的頭髮，這讓我很生氣。

work against

bú lì
不利

 例句 -

Your voluminous dress works against
the dance.

你寬鬆的裙子不利跳舞。

work on

gǎi shàn
改善

374

 例句 -

Miss Yeung says I need to work on my handwriting.

楊老師說我要改善我的字跡。

work out¹

duàn liàn shēn tǐ
鍛煉身體

例句 -

In order to keep in good shape, he works out in the gym twice a week.

為了保持良好身材，他每星期到健身房鍛煉兩次。

work out²

chéng xiào lǐ xiǎng

成效理想

 例句 --------

Dad invented an automatic watering system and it worked out well.

爸爸發明了自動灑水系統，成效十分理想。

work out³

jì suàn
計算

例句

This sum is too hard that I cannot work it out.

這道數學題太難了，我算不出來。

wrap up
chuān de nuǎn huo
穿得暖和

 例句 -

It is snowing. Do not forget to wrap up.

現在正在下雪，別忘了穿上保暖衣服。

write back

huí xìn
回信

例句 ------------------------------

I received a gift with a letter from my friend. I am writing her back to thank her.

我收到了朋友寄來的禮物和信件。我正在回信向她道謝。

zip up

lā shàng lā liàn
拉上拉鍊

 例句 ----------------------------------

Mum, please zip up the wetsuit for me.

媽媽，請幫我拉上潛水衣的拉鍊。

zoom in

fàng dà huà miàn
放大畫面

 例句 ------------------------

You have to zoom in on the lead singer.

你要拉近鏡頭，對準樂隊主唱來拍攝。

新雅兒童英文圖解字典
片語動詞

作　　者：Elaine Tin
繪　　圖：歐偉澄
責任編輯：黃稔茵
美術設計：劉麗萍
出　　版：新雅文化事業有限公司
　　　　　香港英皇道499號北角工業大廈18樓
　　　　　電話：（852）2138 7998
　　　　　傳真：（852）2597 4003
　　　　　網址：http://www.sunya.com.hk
　　　　　電郵：marketing@sunya.com.hk
發　　行：香港聯合書刊物流有限公司
　　　　　香港荃灣德士古道220-248號荃灣工業中心16樓
　　　　　電話：（852）2150 2100
　　　　　傳真：（852）2407 3062
　　　　　電郵：info@suplogistics.com.hk
印　　刷：中華商務彩色印刷有限公司
　　　　　香港新界大埔汀麗路36號
版　　次：二〇二三年十一月初版

版權所有·不准翻印

ISBN: 978-962-08-8234-0
©2023 Sun Ya Publications (HK) Ltd.
18/F, North Point Industrial Building, 499 King's Road, Hong Kong
Published in Hong Kong SAR, China
Printed in China

作者簡介

Elaine Tin 田依莉

　　持有翻譯及傳譯榮譽文學士學位和語文學碩士學位，曾任兒童圖書翻譯及編輯。熱愛英文教學，喜與兒童互動，故於二零一四年成為英文導師，把知識、經驗和興趣結合起來，讓學生愉快地學習。她認為每個孩子都是獨特的，如能在身旁陪伴和輔助，就能激發他們的興趣和潛質。著有英文學習書《LEARN and USE English in Context 活學活用英文詞彙大圖典》及《中英成語有文化 IDIOMS AND PHRASES》。後者榮獲第三屆香港出版雙年獎「語文學習組別最佳出版獎」。

繪者簡介

Jonas Au 歐偉澄

　　喜歡畫畫、甜品和冷笑話的平凡上班族。

　　目標是可以在發展興趣的同時，能夠應付現在和將來的生活。希望自己的畫作能同時為自己和別人帶來一點快樂和幸福感，透過繪畫留住美好時刻和表達對未來的期盼。

　　目前正在尋找屬於自己的繪畫風格和克服畏高症。